THE SPIDER WEAVER

A Legend of Kente Cloth

BY
Margaret Musgrove

ILLUSTRATED BY
Julia Cairns

SCHOLASTIC INC.
New York Toronto London Auckland Sydney
Mexico City New Delhi Hong Kong Buenos Aires

This book was originally published in hardcover by
the Blue Sky Press in 2001.

ISBN 0-590-98794-1

Copyright © 2001 by Margaret Musgrove
Illustrations copyright © 2001 by Julia Cairns
All rights reserved.
Published by Scholastic Inc.
SCHOLASTIC and associated logos are trademarks
and/or registered trademarks of Scholastic Inc.

18 17 16 15 14 13 12 11 10   8 9 10 11 12 / 0

Printed in the U.S.A.   08

First Scholastic paperback printing, February 2002

Designed by Kathleen Westray

To Taura and Derek,
with faith in Romans 8:28
— M. M.

For my mother, with love
— J. C.

Koragu and Ameyaw were returning home when
Ameyaw stopped suddenly. The light from his
lantern had fallen on an amazing sight, glowing
like moonbeams against the midnight sky.

"Come look, my friend," Ameyaw whispered to
Koragu. "I see a small miracle."

The small miracle was actually a web. But never before
had either of them seen such a wondrous design! Yet it
had been woven with a single unbroken thread—a thread
that was even finer than a strand of human hair.

"Let's bring this treasure home with us to study,"
Koragu whispered to Ameyaw.

Ameyaw carefully detached the web from where it held fast to a banana tree. But as he did, the web collapsed, sticking to his fingers.

"Oh, it is ruined!" Koragu cried. "Now how will
we ever learn to weave this beautiful design?"
Saddened, the weavers walked home. Their
discovery was lost forever.

When the men entered their village at dawn, Ameyaw's wife, Afiya, came out to meet them.

Afiya offered them a calabash filled with cool water to drink.

Neither man spoke as he ate, and for this reason Afiya could sense that something was wrong.

"Please, tell me what troubles you," she said.

"It is a beautiful web," her husband answered sadly. "When we tried to bring it home from the forest to study, it crumpled in my hands and was ruined."

"Do you think you can find another one like it?" Afiya asked quietly. Koragu was doubtful. "This web was very different—very special. And no creature *ever* spins the same web twice."

"Perhaps what happened was a blessing," Afiya suggested gently. "Though you cannot find the same web again, perhaps you can find the same weaver."

And that is what Koragu and Ameyaw set out to do.
Early the next morning, they eagerly made their
way through the bush.

Past the tall silk cottons and papaya trees, they found the banana tree where they had first seen the extraordinary web.

Sure enough, in front of them were the beginnings
of a new masterpiece.
In no time, a slender black leg emerged from
the shadows and rested lightly on the silk threads.

Ameyaw and Koragu could see the creature clearly
now: The Master Web Weaver was a lovely, large,
yellow-and-black spider.

As soon as they saw the spider, the men felt terrible for
wrecking the magnificent web the night before. Now they
could see that the web was the beautiful spider's home.
Longing to take the web home with them, the weavers

looked at each other. But neither of them wanted to destroy the spider's home a second time. They were about to leave when the spider looked directly at them and began a weaving dance.

Dip! Twist. Turn and glide. The spider made her way across and back over the web. She moved like a woman dancing, regal and very graceful.

The spider wove on and on into the afternoon, and the weavers stood still in admiration as they watched her.
At dusk, the tired but satisfied spider completed her creation.

The spider moved sideways to the edge of her web. But before disappearing into the shadows, she turned in the direction of Ameyaw and Koragu. In that brief moment, the men were quite certain she smiled at them.

Then, in the blink of an eye, she was gone.
The beautiful spider had shown the weavers how to
weave new, intricate designs. What a wonderful teacher
she had been! What a wonderful gift she had given them!

With great joy they returned to their village.
In time, the weavers redesigned their looms so they
could imitate the spider's weaving dance. At first,
they copied her patterns in black and white thread,

but soon they dyed their threads in bright colors and developed many new patterns themselves. And they named this new woven cloth *kente-nwen-ntoma*— what today is commonly called kente cloth.

Everyone in the village wanted to wear this new cloth, but, at first, only the king of the Ashanti people wore it on special occasions. As time passed, others were allowed to wear the new cloth, too.

Soon the two weavers were well known across
Ghana. And, because of the spider's generous gift,
they created designs and patterns that are still worn
throughout the world today.

AFTERWORD

The story in this book is widely known among the weavers in Ghana and dates back to the mid-seventeenth century during the time of King Oti Akenten. Today, kente cloth is worn all over the world, but most often by heads of state in different African countries. Even now, certain patterns are reserved for the Ashanti king. Ashanti chiefs will carry extra kente when they are called together by the king. If they are wearing a pattern the king has chosen, they must immediately remove it and select another kente.

In the United States of America and other countries with people of African descent, kente is often worn as a statement of pride in African heritage. Students frequently wear a strip of kente on their gowns when they graduate. Some fraternities and sororities have their Greek letters and colors woven into kente strips.

Machine-woven kente is less expensive than the handmade cloth, but it is also less refined, and the colors are less vibrant. Kente is a beautiful and extremely expensive cloth. People almost never cut the strips of kente to make shirts or skirts. Instead, they wear one strip alone or many strips sewn together, making yards of kente cloth to drape around the body.

Many patterns woven in kente cloth have significance. All of the traditional old patterns have meanings which, for the most part, are proverbs. "One man cannot rule a country" is one of the translations. When heads of state and other dignitaries visit Ghana, often original kente designs are made for these visitors.

In the Ashanti region of Ghana, you can still see yellow, red, and blue threads laid out to dry in the sun. There are fine, handmade looms and *asase-ntoma*—apprentice weavers—who learn to gather their own dyes and process yarns for weaving kente.

And like their masters, and their masters' masters before them, they are told the story of how a beautiful spider shared her weaving secrets with two resourceful, expert weavers.

And how she gave us the remarkable gift of kente one day long, long ago.

PRONUNCIATION GUIDE

Kente *ken*-tee	Nana Ameyaw naa-*naa* aa-may-*yow*
Ashanti a-*shan*-tee	Nwen-ntoma *nnwen*-un-*toe*-ma
Bonwire bon-*weer*-ay	Afiya aa-*fee*-yaa
Ghana *gaa*-naa	Kente nwen-ntoma *ken*-tee *nnwen*-un-*toe*-ma
Nana Koragu naa-*naa kor*-ay-guu	Asase-ntoma aa-*saa*-say-un-*toe*-ma